O. Whillikers in the

Hall of Champions

By Former L.A. Laker

Jay Carty

with Phil Nash

Illustrations by Norm Daniels

Gospel Light
Ventura, California, U.S.A.

Published by Gospel Light
Ventura, California, U.S.A.
Printed in Singapore

Gospel Light is an evangelical Christian publisher dedicated to serving the leaders and families of the local church. It is our prayer that this book will help you discover biblical truth for your own life and help you meet the needs of others. May God richly bless you.

For a free catalog of resources from Gospel Light, please call your Christian supplier or contact us at 1-800-4-GOSPEL *or* www.gospellight.com.

LIBRARY OF CONGRESS CATALOGING-IN-PUBLICATION DATA
Carty, Jay.
  O. Whillikers in the Hall of Champions / Jay Carty, with Phil Nash; illustrations by Norm Daniels.
   p. cm.
  Summary: Hugh Mills the marlin, Rippy Tance the porpoise, and six other sea creatures demonstrate the value of humility, repentance, and other godly character traits.
  ISBN 0-8307-2634-9 (trade paper)
  [1. Christian life—Fiction. 2. Conduct of life—Fiction. 3. Marine animals—Fiction.] I. Nash, Phil.
  II. Daniels, Norm, ill. III. Title.

  PZ7.C25175 Ow 2000
  [Fic]—dc21   00-024523

1 2 3 4 5 6 7 8 9 10 11 12 13 14 15 / 05 04 03 02 01 00

Rights for publishing this book in other languages are contracted by Gospel Literature International (GLINT). GLINT also provides technical help for the adaptation, translation and publishing of Bible study resources and books in scores of languages worldwide. For further information, contact GLINT at P.O. Box 4060, Ontario, CA 91761-1003, U.S.A. You may also send e-mail to Glintint@aol.com, or visit the GLINT website at www.glint.org.

To my daughter, Kim, my firstborn.
I know of no one who better exemplifies the
character qualities of the Beatitudes.

To my son, John, whom I love with all my heart.
He has taught me what it means to be loyal.
I am aware of no one who knows
how to be a better friend.

To Darryl DelHousaye, pastor of Scottsdale Bible Church.
I was listening to his tapes on the Beatitudes during a
late-night drive from Hume Lake to Oregon
when I got the idea for O. Whillikers.

In memory of Lorene (Low Gear) Worsham,
a dear friend and winner of the Uncle Ernie Award.
She provided shelter for Toad Lee Purrhart when he needed it the most.
I miss her.

Special thanks to Sarah Hemingway, Kim Hayashi,
Bob Morris, Sue Morris and John Stout.

Contents

A Note to Parents and Teachers 7

Chapter 1 12
The Tale of Hugh Mills, the Humble Marlin

Chapter 2 20
The Tale of Rippon Tance, a Porpoise with a Purpose

Chapter 3 33
The Tale of Jim Teal, the Mean Moray Eel

Chapter 4 46
The Tale of the Samoan Stingrays, the To-Do-Wright Brothers

Chapter 5 59
The Tale of Harvey Mertzy, the Merciful Mollusk

Chapter 6 72
The Tale of Toad Lee Purrhart, a Toad with a Pure Heart

Chapter 7 85
The Tale of Peaz Maukkar, the Peacemaker

Chapter 8 98
The Tale of Percy Q. T. Cod, a Persecuted Codfish

From the Living Sea Scrolls 111

God Said It Like This for You and Me 112

A Note to Parents and Teachers

The Beatitudes describe character qualities that Jesus said result from true faith. The eight stories in this book bring the Beatitudes to life by showing kids who had it tough, but who learned to be godly in spite of their circumstances. Our past cannot be used as an excuse for ungodliness. This book was written to help kids avoid that trap.

Over half the children in America are from disrupted homes. I wish they all could take a trip through the Hall of Champions. I wrote this book for them. But *O. Whillikers* will help kids from traditional families, too. In these pages, young people from all backgrounds will find a new appreciation for their friends who aren't so fortunate.

As you read *O. Whillikers* with your child, when the book asks a question, make sure to wait for your child's answer. A picture of Little Stevie Stop Scallop will remind you. Let the stories launch a conversation between the two of you. If you end up talking longer than planned, or if your younger child gets too sleepy before finishing the story, you can always continue the next day.

Children young and old will learn the eight Beatitudes when they stop to think and answer the questions at the beginning and end of each story.

You'll find that both you and your child will look forward to your trips through the Hall of Champions—and that some of the godly character from O. Whillikers' friends will rub off with each visit.

Hi! I'm O. Whillikers, and I'm a walrus.

Jumpin' G. Whillikers was my dad. Ahh Whillikers was my grandpa. And William Wadsworth Whillikers was my great-grandfather. I come from a long line of Whillikers. They were all critters with good character. I've had good examples to follow.

O. Whillikers is my name and stories are my game.

I'm going to tell you eight tales, or stories. These are no ordinary lobster tails. These are tales about seafolk who are legends around these parts. Their pictures hang right here in Bea and Atta Tude's Hall of Champions. Why? Because each of them had *character*.

You'll find eight portraits in the Tude's Hall of Champions, and I will tell you a story about each one.

As you read, do me a favor. When I ask you a question, stop and answer it right away. Out loud! Little Stevie Stop Scallop  will be there to remind you.

How many pictures hang in Bea and Atta Tude's Hall of Champions? If you can't remember, turn back a page to remind yourself. Don't read any further until you get the right answer. Remember, little Stevie is watching.

Now it's time for a lobster tail! Oops! I mean our first *tale*.

The Tale of Hugh Mills, the Humble Marlin

Our first story is about a kind of fish called a marlin. This tale is about a marlin named Hugh Mills.

Mean Marvelous Marvin and Slammin' Sammy Shellfish were two of the baddest dudes under the sea. One day they were hangin' out when Slammin' Sammy saw a chance for a little fun.

"Hey, Marv, check it out! It's a school of wimpy nerd fish. I'm itchin' to do some tail kickin'. You moosh, mash and mangle 'em. I'll do the chompin', stompin' and clobberin'!"

"Great idea, Sammy. You're one selfish shellfish. I'm all *over* that. Let's do it!"

"It sure is fun being a bad-dude-fish," Slammin' Sammy said gleefully.

"Yeah, but bein' the baddest is hard work," Marvelous Marvin reminded him. "It's not easy keeping everyone scared of us. We're gonna need help. Hey, it's time we got our little brothers in on this! You grab Skinflint and I'll get Hugh."

"Slammin' Sammy and Skinflint Shellfish—the Meanie Brothers. I like the sound of that. But you might have trouble talking your brother into joining us. Hugh's a different kinda dude."

Suddenly, Marvelous Marvin and Slammin' Sammy found themselves surrounded by carp cars. The sea police! The terrible twosome tried to flee the scene, but it was too late. The carps arrested them and hauled them before Judge Judy Gavelfish. She sent Marvin and Sammy up the river to do time for terrifying townfish.

Lots of kid-fish look up to their older brothers and sisters and want to be just like them. Skinflint Shellfish wanted to be just like Slammin' Sammy. But even though Hugh Mills loved his big brother Marvin, he didn't want to grow up to be like him. Hugh wasn't into scaring and hurting others.

Have you ever noticed how some kids at your school are mean to others? That's the way it was at Hugh's school, too. The bully fish would tease his friends.

"Hey, check out Lois Lottafish. Hubba hubba, tubbafish!"

"Watch out for Tommy Turkeyfish. He'll gobble your lunch grub."

"Yo, Clara Clam. What a loser!"

But Hugh Mills was a kind marlin. "Hi Clara! You look a little down. I heard the kids calling you names again. Is that why you hide in your shell when anyone comes around?"

"Well, Hugh, I feel so shy. I just clam up around the other fish."

"But Clara, I think you're wonderful! The Fishmaker knew exactly what He was doing when He made you, and He did a great job! There's not another clam in the sea like you."

"Really? Hugh, you make me feel so good about myself. Lois, isn't Hugh the best?"

"Oh, yes! Most of the other kid-fish say mean things to me just because I'm heavy. It hurts my feelings a lot, even though I pretend it doesn't. Anyway, Hugh's right, Clara. You sure are nice when you open up."

Hugh said, "You see?! What's on the outside doesn't matter. It's what's on the inside that *really* counts. And both of you are terrific!"

As Lois, Clara and Hugh entered the fisheteria at lunchtime, Tommy Turkeyfish could be heard above all the other noise in the room. He was burpy, slurpy, messy, sloppy and talked with his mouth full.

"I like those little wormy things on the bottom. Yummmm! You're not going to eat those kelp chips are you? May I have a couple of your tofu fish goos?" Tommy slurped them up.

"Oh, gross!" said Lois. "It's Tommy Turkeyfish! He always calls me names. And when he does, he spits food all over the place."

"Don't let him bother you, Lois. He only eats like that because he doesn't know what else to do. Did you know that Tommy's folks fight a lot? He has it real rough at home."

"I didn't know. That's too bad."

"What he really needs is a friend. Let's ask him to swim with us to check out what's happening over at the reef. I think the Rockfish are jammin' today."

"But I don't like him. He's so messy!"

"Come on, Lois. He's really lonely inside. Remember what I told you? He needs friends."

"Oh, all right, I guess we could ask him to come. I'll try to be nice."

"That's the spirit! Hey Tommy, do you want to swim over to the reef with us?"

"Who, me? Well, sure. I mean, I guess so. Say, do they have any-thing to eat there?"

One day the county kingfish hosted a dinner to honor a few of the community's finest fish. Slammin' Sammy's little brother Skinflint Shellfish went with his friend Paul Pufferfish to show off and mooch free food.

"Hey, Paul, it's a great party now that we're here!" Skinflint shouted as they entered the room.

Paul puffed himself up with pride. "Yeah, we're the greatest!"

"Hey, Pufferdude. You need to strut and swagger more when you swim. Watch me and do like I do."

Together they pushed their way to the front of the room. They threw Sidney Sea Snake and Sylvester Slug out of the way and grabbed the chairs on either side of the kingfish's seat. The new terrible twosome took the seats of honor for themselves.

"Okay, here comes the kingfish," Paul Pufferfish preened. "We'll be cool next to him. He's gonna like sittin' with us."

Skinflint saw someone he knew sitting far from the head table. "Look there! It's Hugh Mills. He ain't cool. He's sittin' all the way in the back. That's a good place for him."

His Majesty Karl Kingfish the Great was the grandest grouper in the grotto. And he always carried a super-duper grouper scooper for occasions just like this. Seeing how rude Skinflint and his friend the pufferfish were being, the king scooped them up and flung them all the way to the back wall of the hall.

The motley pair grunted and cried as they hit the wall with a *thump* and a *squish*.

"Umph!" said Paul.

"Ouch!" said Skinflint.

Karl Kingfish the Great spoke in a regal voice. "Will the marlin seated in the back come up here and sit by me? I want to introduce my friend, Hugh Mills—the best helper and encourager in this county!"

Everyone cheered with shouts of "You're right!" "Good call!" "Right on!" "Bravo!" "Great choice!" "Hugh's the best!"

"Clara Clam," the kingfish said, "did you have something you wanted to say?"

"Yes, I do, Your Majesty. Hugh Mills helped me to open up. And he helped Lois Lottafish and Tommy Turkeyfish, too."

"He sure did," said Lois. "Hugh showed me that it's what we are on the inside that counts."

Tommy added, "Hugh wanted to be my friend when I didn't have any friends."

The kingfish said, "Thank you, Lois and Tommy. And thank you to all who came to honor Hugh Mills tonight! I'd say that includes just about everyone, except maybe those two critters stuck to the back wall!"

The kingfish turned to Hugh. "Hugh, please accept this shiny gold medal with our gratitude. I'll read what it says: *To the most humble citizen in Kingfish County*. And that's not all. Fish University has named a word after you and put it in the dictionary:

Humility . . . a Hugh Mills word.

"People who boast and bluster try to lift themselves up by putting others down and by calling attention to themselves. But those with Hugh-Mill-ity feel good about how The Fishmaker has made them. And they want to help others—just like you do!

"As the kingfish, I hereby make a proclamation: The Fishmaker made us and loves us. That makes us all valuable. From now on, when you help others to feel loved and valued, we shall call it 'doing a Hugh.'"

Hugh Mills thought for a moment about putting on the medal and strutting in front of the other fish. But he didn't. Instead, he put the medal on his wall where he alone could see and enjoy it. He didn't flash it around town to make his neighbors envious. You see, Hugh Mills really was a humble marlin.

Can you remember the last time you acted selfish or proud?

When is the last time you acted humble like Hugh?

What was the word that was named after Hugh Mills?

What does it mean to "do a Hugh"?

Well, our first tale is over—but there are seven more. Now it's time to talk to God. Why don't you pray and tell Him about the last time you were selfish? Then ask Him to help you be more like Hugh Mills.

You can feel good about how God made you. You are unique and very special to Him. And you can help others feel good about how God made them, too. Would you do that right now?

The Tale of Rippon Tance, a Porpoise with a Purpose

Hi! O. Whillikers here. I have a great tail, er, story for you! But before I tell it, let's think back to our last tale. What was the word that best described Hugh Mills?

Our next hall-of-famer from the Hall of Champions is a porpoise who made some bad choices and did some bad things. But as we will see, that didn't make him a bad porpoise. In fact, he ended up making some very *good* choices.

RIPPON Preston Tance

Rippon Preston Tance was named after his famous grandporp, Colonel Preston Tance. The Colonel had led the Royal Dolphin Lancers against the Liverpool Sharks, a sea gang that terrorized the coast of England years ago. The Lancers did some jaws rippin' and cleaned up the coastline. The Colonel named his son Lance in their honor, and Lance named his son Rippon to remember the Lancers' deeds.

Like his grandfather, Rippon Tance was a porpoise with a purpose. He desperately longed to be liked. And he thought the way to make pals was to be like everyone else and do what they did.

One day, Rippon swam into the shady but popular Gilbert Gill.

"Wassup, Rippy?" Gil greeted him. "Say, where'd you get a name like Rippy anyway?"

"It's short for Rippon. Kids in school used to make fun of me and call me names like Prissy Porpoise and Dumbbell Dolphin. Fish, I hated those names! Once some crab called me Rippy, and I thought it sounded kind of cool. At least it was better than the other stuff."

"Hey, Rippy's cool. Say, how come I never see your dad around?"

"My dad died in a tuna rescue operation when I was two."

"Too bad, dude! What's with your mom?"

"She works at SeaWorld to support us. It's been hard since my dad died. I come home every day to an empty pool. And my mom worries about the kind of friends I make."

Gil smiled. "Well, she's not around now, so let me introduce you to Eddie the Eel, Larry Lightfingers Lingcod and Crawford Crayfish. I gotta go, but you'll like hangin' with these guys. Check it out. There they are."

TEST TODAY

"Yo, Eddie the Eel! This here is Rippy. He's a smooth dude. Can you show him what's cool around school?"

"No problem! Rippy, I'll show you how to sneak peeks at Brilliant Beulah Butterfish's papers during tests. You'll get a good grade and be slick as an eel."

Larry Lightfingers Lingcod snickered. "Then we'll lift some licorice and lighters when we go trolling for gum and grouper gulps at the DeepSix."

"Crawford Crayfish, I'm surprised you showed," Gil said. "You said you would, but we never know with you. You'd rather lie about your own name than tell the truth."

"Life's more fun when you keep 'em guessin'," said the crafty crustacean. "A few fibs a day make you say 'Hey, hey!' I'll teach you to tell some real whoppers, Rippy. Your mom'll go for 'em hook, line and sinker."

"I don't know . . . I've never lied to my mom."

"Get a life, fish! I don't know a sardine who doesn't try to smoke his folks."

Rippy's mom knew that we end up becoming like the characters we hang with. I guess that's how Rippy came to lose some of his good character. Character is something everyone else can see in you, but you can only see it when you look in a mirror. And it's easy to get holes in your character when your friends don't have much.

Do your friends have good character?

What might happen to you if they don't?

Rippy had made some bad choices in friends, just because he wanted to be liked. But his story isn't finished yet. Let's see what happened the very next day at school in Mrs. Orca's class.

"All right, everyone, it's time for our test." Mrs. Orca called the class to order. "Let's see what you've learned. There isn't enough room for everyone to be separated by a desk. Rippy, I can trust you. Would you sit next to Brainy Bob Bass?"

Rippy had spent the evening hanging out with his new friends and hadn't studied. *I'm not sure of the answers*, he thought. *What would Eddie the Eel do?*

All it took was a few sneaky peeks when Mrs. Orca wasn't looking. Rippy was sure he would get a great grade now.

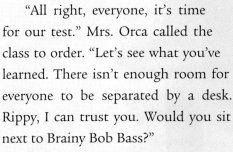

That afternoon Rippy went home and looked in the mirror. "Oh no, I've got holes in my character!" he cried.

Rippy didn't like the looks of this. Sure, he would get a good grade on the test, but he wasn't sure that losing his good character was worth it.

The next day Rippy and his mom were driving down the seaway. "We need to stop at the Shells station," she said. "While we're there, let's go into the DeepSix Mart and get a half-gallon of skim chum and some frozen worm concentrate for juice in the morning."

Rippy followed. He didn't have any money, but he sure did want some gum.

Then he remembered what Larry Lightfingers had said. So he looked around to make sure nobody was watching, and before he really even thought about it, he stuffed a pack of cod-liver-flavored Fishilicious in his blowhole and walked out. No-body knew—except Rippy, of course.

But that evening Rippon Preston Tance took another look in the mirror. He wasn't very proud of what he saw. "I don't think a pack of Fish-ilicious was worth this," he said to no one in particular.

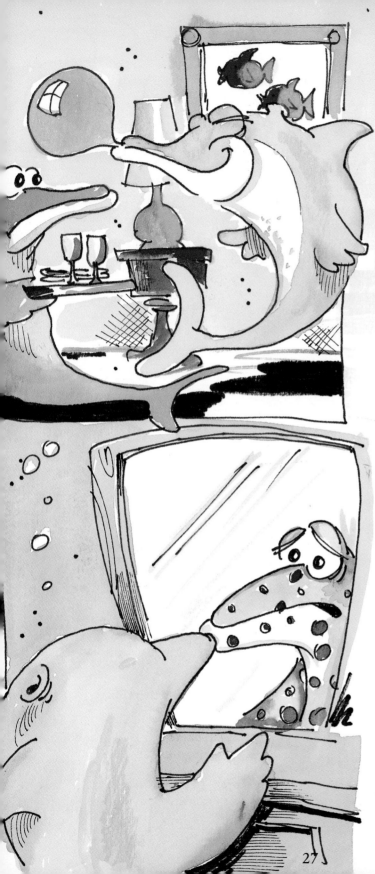

After dinner, Rippy was chewing a piece of his ill-gotten gum when his mother asked, "Where did you get the gum?"

"At the store."

"Where did you get money for gum? I thought you spent your allowance . . ."

"I found a dollar on the ground at school." The lie slipped out easily. "I took it to the principal, but when no one claimed it at the end of the day, he let me keep it."

Rippy's mother believed his lie.

Porpoises can be real smart when they need to be, Rippy kidded himself. Then he thought about Crawford. *I did what he would have done. I lied to my mom.*

On the way to bed that night, Rippy looked in the mirror. There was hardly any good character left at all! His lie had cost just as much as cheating and stealing. Rippy knew he had made The Fishmaker sad.

Rippy's mom had to work that Saturday. He had been given a list of chores to do, but his new friends had other plans. Rippy was sweeping the porch when they showed up.

"Grab your seahorse," Eddie said. "We're goin' to the kelp forest in the cove."

"But I'm not supposed to . . ."

"Hey, come on, fish! Your mom's never gonna know. Besides, Crawford can always come up with a cover story. Ain't that right?"

"Buuurrrp! Uh, sure."

So Rippy dropped his broom, and they all took off for the cove. It was getting easier all the time for Rippy to disobey.

When they got to the forest, Eddie said, "Hey, Fingers, look over there. Isn't that Wally Walrus takin' swimmin' lessons? What a wimp!"

"Hey, blubber gut!" Larry shouted. "How's the water? Or maybe I should say, 'How's the bottom?'"

"Don't your teeth get in the way when you're tryin' to do the breast stroke?" Crawford cackled. "Hey, Rippy, it's your turn to rag on Wally. Roast him good!"

Everyone was laughing and having a good time at Wally's expense. Everyone but Rippy. He remembered all too well what it was like to be called names.

28

"Hey Rippy! How come you didn't say nothin'?"

"My throat's kinda sore, Eddie. I couldn't talk very loud." Rippy didn't like what was goin' down, but he felt caught in the middle.

Crawford went on teasing Wally. "Hey, Wally, I'll race you to the other side. We know what a good swimmer you must be 'cause you're takin' lessons, so you have to swim with Eddie the Eel wrapped around you!"

The bullies were laughing and pushing Wally when Rippy finally took a stand.

"I don't think we should be pickin' on Wally. Let him go!"

"Are you crazy?" Eddie asked, dumbfounded. "What are you doin'?"

"What do you care what we do to him?" Crawford demanded.

"I'm not sure . . . but I do care. So let him go!" Rippy stood tall and flexed his porp-pecs.

Eddie, Larry and Crawford let go of Wally, gawking with gaping gills. They stood fin-to-fin and started to make a move on their former friend. But one look at Rippy's purposeful porp-puss made them think twice. They backed away and turned to leave, but all three had something to say as they left.

"Let that prissy porpoise play with the wimp. Let's go!"

"Dumbbell dolphin! He's all yours. And you can forget about bein' part of our crew."

"Don't call us and we won't call you. We're outta here!"

Eddie, Larry and Crawford jumped on their seahorses and made tracks for home.

Being called names didn't hurt Rippy this time. He could feel his good character coming back.

The next day Rippy went to his teacher, Mrs. Orca, and confessed everything. "I cheated on the test," he told her. "You can give me an F or let me take it again. I'll take what's coming to me, but I want my good character back."

Good ol' Mrs. Orca gave Rippy another chance. She really wasn't the killer whale everyone thought she was.

Rippy then went to the DeepSix Mart at the Shells station and talked to the owner, Sam Squid. "I am a shoplifter," he confessed. "I pinched a pack of gum. You can call the police if you want to, but I promise to save my allowance and pay you back next week. Or you can give me something to do to work off my debt. It's your choice. I'll take what I have coming to me. I want to be able to look in the mirror and like what I see."

Sam gave Rippy a broom and snarled, "Sweep the floor and empty the trash. Do that and we'll call it even." Sam scowled, but inside he was smiling because he admired Rippy's courage and good character.

Rippy was making some good choices.

That evening, when his mother came home after a tough day at SeaWorld, Rippy made her day by admitting his lie.

"I'm sorry I lied to you, Mom. Please forgive me. I'll try my best not to do it again." Then he headed for the mirror.

Rippy stood a little straighter when he saw that most of his character was back. He had made things right with Mrs. Orca, Sam Squid and his mom. There was only one more to go. So he prayed and asked The Fishmaker to forgive him. When he looked up again, there were no holes at all. He really was a porpoise with a purpose.

There is a word for what Rippy did. Fish University named it after him and put it in *Merriam-Lobster's Under-the-Bridge Dictionary:*

Repentance . . . a Rippy Tance word.

Repentance is what you do when you've lost your good character and want to get it back.

You repent by confessing what you did wrong and then doing your best to make it right and deciding deep down inside not to do it again.

Repentance is doing what Rippy Tance did.

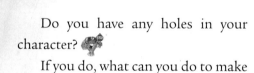

Do you have any holes in your character?

If you do, what can you do to make right what you did wrong?

Is there anything you need to confess to your folks?

What is the word named after Rippy Tance?

Why not pray right now and talk to God about the stuff you've done that has cost some of your good character. He'll forgive you and you'll feel a lot better about yourself. Then just like Rippy Tance, you'll get your character back!

The Tale of Jim Teal, the Mean Moray Eel

This story is about Jim Teal and it's a dandy! I think you'll like it a lot. But first, let's think back to our first two stories. What word means to be humble and not a showoff? It sounds like the name of our friend Hugh.

Now think of a word that means to turn from doing wrong and start doing right. It sounds like the name of our buddy Rippy. What is the word?

Our third story begins in the kitchen where Jim Teal, a moray eel, is talking with his Aunt Lucille.

"Aunt Lucille, I sure am glad that you and Uncle Morrie took me in. I like living here a lot more than those foster homes. But you seem real sad sometimes. Have I done something wrong?"

"Oh, gracious no, Jim! It's just that your Uncle Morrie is drinking a lot. Especially when he's with Grandpa Murray. They get so loud. Like right now. They're in there watching that Super Fishbowl game on television. Every critter in the cove can hear them! At first they're kind of funny, but it doesn't take long until the two become rude and crude—and mean. And then they always cause a scene. Too many suds will do that to Morrie."

Jim had heard stories about his uncle. A moray eel looks ferocious with its big mouth and sharp teeth. Uncle Morrie liked to hide behind rocks and scare the slime out of other sea creatures. Like he did when he overheard Samuel Salmon say, "Lurking in holes and jumping out, scaring people to death—nobody likes that."

When Morrie heard that, he rearranged Sam's mouth. It took an oral sturgeon to straighten his teeth.

Fish, like people, usually do what's expected of them. Expect their best and you'll get their best. Expect the worst and that's usually what you'll get. That's the way it was with Uncle Morrie. People expected him to act the way he looked—to live up to his reputation as a bad-dude-fish. So he did. Morrie Teal was one mean moray eel. So mean, in fact, that Aunt Lucille Teal had to put Morrie out of the house.

"Jim, I'm sorry that Uncle Morrie is not around to help you anymore, but his drinking has just made life too hard. I asked him to get a room at the Coral Cave Inn."

"I understand, Aunt Lucille. I'm sorry for you, too! Uncle Morrie was just too mean. One day, I heard him call Harry Hake a blankety-blank and Big Mac Mackerel a so-and-so for no reason! Then he proceeded to whup their tails. It was awful. Did he hit you, too?"

"Sometimes," said Aunt Lucille. "So he had to go."

In some ways, life was easier without Uncle Morrie in the house. But it was harder, too. After all, a young eel needs an older eel to teach him how to grow up to become a good eel. Jim was having a tough time without someone to show him the right way. His Aunt Lucille was worried about him.

Get off my case

"Jim, I'm concerned about you," she said one day. "You seem to be having trouble at school and with friends. Last week, I overheard a sand shark tell Barry Cuda to stay out of your way. He said you're one bad fish and that you like feeling rough and tough and angry. Jim, is that true? What is happening? Is there anything I can do to help?"

"Nah! I'm okay. 'Bad' means good, and I'm good 'n' bad!"

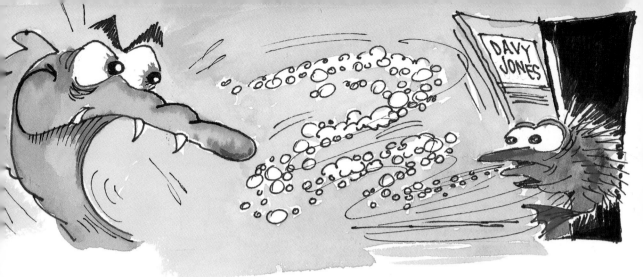

Jim was becoming too much like his Uncle Morrie. Aunt Lucille could see it. She decided to call Principal Pipefish and get the scoop on the real eel.

The principal had plenty to say—none of it good. "Last Tuesday, Barney Blowfish was casually cruising down the hall when Jim jumped out of a doorway and scared the air right out of him. Barney looked like somebody had turned a balloon loose. Pfffhhewwww! What a racket it made when he flew into Davey Jones's locker!

"On Wednesday, Jim mashed Margaret Mussel's mustard on Paul Pike's pizza and Betty Bumfish's biscuits during lunch. Mustard squirted everywhere and all over everyone. Jim laughed while the girls cried. Paul Pike didn't want to get punched so he plugged his puckered pout and kept quiet.

"And poor Tilly Tushfish? At recess during a game of tootsie toss, Jim Teal turned traitor to his team and intentionally tossed his tootsie at Tilly. It stuck on her tushie as she turned tail and took off. How embarrassing for Tilly! That happened on Thursday."

"I'm worried about Jim" said Aunt Lucille. "He's becoming a mean moray eel."

Aunt Lucille knew she needed help with Jim, so she called Morrie's brother Ernie Eel. Ernie was electric. Nobody messed with him. His jolt was no joke, but he wasn't mean like Morrie and Jim. Ernie was a genuinely gentle electric eel. He had his strength and power under control, and Aunt Lucille knew it.

"Uncle Ernie, I'm having trouble with Jim. He needs a good eel in his life. Would you help?"

"I'd love to, Lucille! I'll take him to the aquarium tomorrow. We'll look at the people and have a chat."

"Hey, Jim, what do you think of the humans?" Ernie asked his nephew.

"Colorful and weird. Mostly weird. What do you think, Uncle Ernie?"

"I think all this people watching has made me hungry. How about some crabcorn? Or a shrimpsicle? I'll have a squid-squirt sundae. And while we're eating, let's take a break and talk."

"Sure, Uncle Ernie, fire away."

"Let me ask you, Jim, did you like the way Uncle Morrie acted when he drank too much?"

"No way! He was rude and crude and loud and mean, and he always caused a scene." Jim shuddered at the memory of his uncle's drinking.

"Then why do you want to be like him?" Uncle Ernie asked.

"What do you mean? I don't drink. I never touch the stuff!"

"I know. But you've developed quite a reputation for being rude and crude and loud and mean, and you love to cause a scene. I heard about what happened at school. Why did you do it?"

"I don't know. I guess I need to live up to my reputation. People expect me to be mean. Besides, I kind of like it when the other fish are afraid of me. It means they've got respect for *this* fish."

"Do you think I am mean?" Ernie asked with a spark in his eye.

"Well, no."

"Do you know any fish with more power than I have?" Ernie's gills crackled.

"No," said Jim, awestruck.

"Then why do you suppose I'm not mean?"

"Only a fool would mess with an electric eel!"

"Do you think fish respect me, even though I don't terrorize them?"

"Sure," Jim said, looking around. "I can see it in their eyes and on their faces."

"Why do you suppose they aren't afraid of me, even though I could hurt them if I wanted?"

"Uncle Ernie, I don't know. What are you trying to tell me?"

"Just this: People may fear you, but that doesn't mean they respect you. You can't demand respect, Jim. You earn respect by being *kind*. Fish who try to demand respect are weak and have holes in their character. They may look strong, but it's what's inside that counts—especially to The Fishmaker. On the inside, bullies and meanies are really weenies and wimps."

That was hard for Jim to hear. He knew he had been acting like a bully. And he knew Uncle Ernie loved him. But his feelings were hurt. Jim Teal hung his head as they swam.

Uncle Ernie finally broke the silence. "I'll bet that crabcorn made you thirsty. How about a soda?"

"Uh, sure. Thanks." After a sip or two, Jim felt a little better. Still he couldn't stop thinking about what Uncle Ernie had said. They swam some more and ended up in a bed of dandyworms. Jim perked up. "I have a blast playing with dandyworms," he said with cruel glee. "It's fun to blow 'em off their stems and watch 'em scatter. Uncle Ernie, look at how all the little worms go when I blow on 'em! Hey, how come none of the worms fell off when *you* touched 'em?"

"Jim, come over here and take a close look, but be very careful this time."

"Wow! All those dandyworms have little faces. And they're smilin'. How come they're doin' that?"

"They aren't afraid," said Uncle Ernie. "They trust me."

But when the dandyworms saw Jim, their smiles turned to looks of terror and they screamed, "Aaggggh! Woooah! Aaggggh! Help us, Ernie!"

"They're not afraid of you, Uncle Ernie. But when they see me, they freak out. Why?"

"You know the answer, Jim."

"Yeah, I guess I do. It's because I'm mean to them."

"Why don't you tell them you're sorry and begin to earn their respect?"

"How will I know when I've got it?"

"When they trust you, then you'll know they respect you."

Jim reached
out and touched the
stem of the dandyworm.
He used his gentlest touch,
but two worms fell off anyhow.
Jim carefully picked them up and
put them back on.

"I'm sorry," he said sincerely. Then he
smiled at the dandyworms, but none smiled back.

Jim kept coming back day after day, smiling
and waiting for the dandyworms to
decide to trust him.

One day, after a few weeks, they
smiled back. Jim had earned their
respect. It was a great day for Jim Teal.

Jim remembered what it was like
when the dandyworms were
frightened of him. Then he
thought of the looks on the
faces of the fish he had bul-
lied at school. He thought, *If
I can win over the dandy-
worms, I can earn the respect
of the fish at school, too. Maybe
we could even
become friends!*

Jim had learned that saying "I'm sorry" was a good start. But he also learned that it takes time to earn trust and respect. So Jim went back to school and began to make things right with all the fish he had been mean to. He started by saying "I'm sorry" to Barney, Margaret, Betty, Paul and Tilly. Then he started working to earn their trust. It took quite a while. But that's the way it is with inside hurts. Inside hurts take a long time to heal. Jim did the best he could to fix the wrong things he had done. He did what Rippy Tance would have done.

From that day on, Jim Teal showed everyone how much better it is to be kind than to be mean. He showed his good character by taking the time to earn the trust of others. And in the end, he got the respect he had always wanted—thanks to the influence of an eel with character like Uncle Ernie.

The Fishmaker was pleased.

Fish University took notice of the changes in Jim Teal, the moray eel. Since he had brought his strength and power under control, the university decided to name a word after him and put it in the dictionary.

Do you know the word that was named after Jim Teal?

Sure.

Gentle . . . a Jim Teal word.

Gentleness does not mean being a coward, a weakling or a wimp. Moray eels are none of those things. But like a trained killer whale at SeaWorld, Jim Teal brought his strength and power under control. That is being gentle.

When was the last time you were mean or hurt people?

Are you mean more than you are gentle?

One more thing: Fish University also began giving an annual Uncle Ernie Award to a fish who helped bad-dude-fish be cool.

Do you know a godly person of good character who could be an Uncle Ernie for you?

What was the word that was named after Jim Teal?

Now, take the time to talk to God about any meanness in you that He would like removed. Then ask Him to show you ways to be more gentle.

Have a nice visit with God!

The Tale of the Samoan Stingrays, the To-Do-Wright Brothers

My trip to the Kingfish County Bank reminded me of our next tale. It's about a couple of twins who had it real tough at home.

Hold it! I almost forgot. We have to do a "think back" first.

What are the names of the three folk we've read about so far? (It's okay to look back at the stories if you need to.)

And what words of character do their names describe?

Done? Okay! Now we're ready.

There are two seafolk in the fourth picture in Bea and Atta Tude's Hall of Fame. Tisno Hooey Too-dooey and Mee Tooey Too-dooey Wright are twin stingrays born in Samoa. And they are known in the Hall of Champions as the To-Do-Wright Brothers.

the To Do Wright Brothers

I first met the To-Do-Wrights at the bank. I had a pocketful of squid, so I stopped to exchange them for a few clams. Have *you* ever tried to stuff a squid into a parking meter? Anyway, there I was, waiting in line, when the notorious Shark Brothers charged through the front door with spearguns drawn.

The leader, Hammerhead, shouted, "This is a stickup! The first fish who moves is sushi. Shovelnose, tell 'em what to do!"

"Cram this case with clams," another shark instructed the turtle teller. "And only the biggest ones! Buzzsaw, get the guard outta the way and watch for carp cars."

"Okay, outta the way, you! Hey, look out for—!"

Just then, a shadowy phantom hammered Hammerhead with a terrible tail. From the other side of the room, a dark shape lunged at Buzzsaw and slammed him to the slab. Then a flashing flipper forced Shovelnose into the bank safe and bolted the door, neatly jailing him inside. It all happened so fast—the sharks didn't know what hit them. The To-Do-Wright Brothers had arrived.

Tisno Hooey and Mee Tooey were officers on the K.I.S.S. Force— that is, the Kingfish's Internal Special Strike Force. Together, they had pretty much eliminated the county's criminal population.

"Well, Mee, it looks like we've done it again."

"You know, Tisno, I never did trust those Sharks. I'm happy to see them in the rice-paddy wagon, headed for the finitentiary."

"They'll make great jail bait."

The Sharks would soon be sharing a cell with the Scumsuckers, who had been convicted of sucking frosting from between the layers of cakes. Birthday parties were pretty flat around these parts until the To-Do-Wrights put an end to their scummy capers.

The beloved brothers had also put an end to the Hell's Angelfish's hassling of the halibut and the haddocks. The Angelfish are now up the river with the other rotten fish—including Barry, Terry and Jerry Cuda, who used to frighten fishfolk on Fourth Street.

The To-Do-Wright twins are known for coming down hard on critters who refuse to do right. But it wasn't always that way. When they were your age, the To-Do-Wrights could have been called the To-Do-*Wrongs*, because they didn't know right from wrong. Life was very confusing and full of double messages for the young stingrays.

"Tisno, do you remember how Dad used to yell at us?" Mee would later say.

"Sure. He used to scream, 'Shut up! Don't yell in the house.'"

"Then he would tell us to go to the store and steal a pack of seaweeds for him. But if we got caught, he'd whip us good!"

"And when I'd cuss, Dad would smack me and say, 'Don't use that kinda language in this house!' And he'd use the same words he told me not to say! Then at parties he would coax us into saying the naughty words so all the older fish would laugh."

Mee said, "I remember when we got caught sneaking a peek at Dad's *Mermaid* magazine, but Dad didn't yell. Instead, he smiled with a gleam in his eye and said, 'Aren't you a little young to be lookin' at that?' Then he left it in plain sight where we could see it."

"It was all so confusing," Tisno agreed. "Life wasn't always easy for us, was it?"

50

"Remember how the other fish at school would stand back and give us plenty of room to swim by because of our stingers?"

"Yeah, we learned early that nobody wanted a touch from our terrible tails. Dad used his on us often enough!"

After the Wright Brothers went to school in the mornings, their dad sold drugs to seedy seafish. At night, after they went to bed, he'd steal stereos and sell them in the canals. They had a bad-dude-fish for a dad.

And their mom? She used the drugs Dad kept around the house. She would disappear for hours, leaving the young brothers to fend for themselves. The Wright home was all wrong.

Good thing for the twins that Mary and Manta Ray lived next door! "They were always so nice to us," Tisno remembered. "When it was cold, Mary Ray would have us in for hot urchin soup. And she made treats like chocolate slug cookies, smooshed snail snacks and frosted kelp cakes. Mmmm!"

"The Rays really loved us," Mee agreed, "and they showed it in so many ways. They were the best!"

"Remember when the police knocked down our front door, Mee? They burst into our cave and Sergeant Sailfish yelled, 'They're in the bedroom!' When they took Mom and Dad away in fincuffs, I was so scared."

"I was scared, too, Tisno! And when they took us downtown to the police station, I was afraid they were going to make us live there."

"Yeah, I remember we just hugged each other and trembled. That was a really hard time."

"I thank The Fishmaker for Mary and Manta Ray!" Mee exclaimed. "I remember them flapping down the hall of the police station. Without saying a word they scooped us up, hugged us hard and took us home with them. I was so glad to see somebody we knew! We didn't know until later that they had permission for us to live with them."

"Tisno, do you remember how different it was living with the Rays?"

"Are you kiddin'? I had to quit cussin' 'cause they didn't allow that kind of language. But they didn't yell at us. They were firm—real firm. And yet they were gentle."

Mee said, "I had to quit smoking and chewing seaweed."

"And I couldn't sneak sips of Suds Light," Tisno agreed. "There wasn't any to sip!"

"And we both had to learn to control our terrible tails. It wasn't easy, but we did it."

O. Whillikers needs to stop the story for a moment and say something to you. I hope you don't mind.

Everybody has something that can hurt a lot more than a stingray's tail. What do you think it is?

A tongue and the words it speaks.

Did you know that words can hurt us in a very deep and lasting way? And just like Tisno and Mee had to learn not to hurt others with their tails, we have to learn not to hurt others with our tongues. Words can do more damage than sticks and stones. Bones heal, but some hurts don't.

Okay! Now back to the boys, who are still reminiscing about the Rays.

"It was different, Mee, not having any naughty books around. But the Rays had some good books—one in particular."

"Yeah, The Fishmaker's Living Sea Scrolls. The Rays read it a lot, and they always read with us at mealtimes and before bed. One night I asked Mary Ray why we read from the Scrolls. I'll never forget what she said: 'Why don't we let you play in the traffic? Is it to spoil your fun?' Tisno, do you remember your answer?"

"Sure! I said, 'It's so we won't get hurt.'"

"And she said, 'That's why we read the Living Sea Scrolls. Doing right helps us not to get hurt, and the Scrolls tell us how to do right.'"

"The Rays helped us so much. They were the best. They always behaved the way they wanted us to behave. We didn't get any double messages in *their* house."

You see, the boys were not bad; they had just learned to do bad things. But thanks to the Rays and the power in the Living Sea Scrolls, the twins were able to break their bad habits and learn to do right. The Fishmaker was very pleased.

Tisno Hooey Too-dooey and Mee Tooey Too-dooey Wright got so good at doing good things that Fish University coined a phrase and put it in their dictionary:

To do right . . . Too-dooey Wright words.

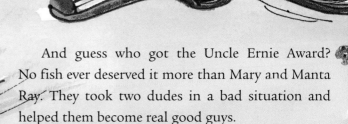

And guess who got the Uncle Ernie Award? No fish ever deserved it more than Mary and Manta Ray. They took two dudes in a bad situation and helped them become real good guys.

What three words are named after the stingray brothers? The brothers learned to control their terrible tails. What do you have to learn to control that can hurt other people?

Fishfolk turn to the Living Sea Scrolls to learn about what's right. Where should you turn to learn what's right?

Are there any confusing double messages in your home? If so, can you talk about them with an adult there? Have you ever used bad words or said mean things to hurt other people? Tell God that you are sorry for the bad stuff or hurtful words you've said. Pray and ask Him to help you control your tongue and do what's right.

Is there anyone you need to tell "I'm sorry for what I said"? Be sure to tell them next time you see them.

And when you pray, don't forget to thank God for both loving and forgiving you. (By now you've probably guessed— He's the real Fishmaker in our stories and the Bible is His book.)

It's been a great day!

I'll talk to you in our next story.

O. Whillikers is outta here!

The Tale of Harvey Mertzy,
the Merciful Mollus

Hey! You must be ready for another story.
But before we get started, let's think back to
the stories we've already read.

Which fish was humble?

Which fish was repentant?

Which eel was gen-teel?

Who were the brothers who did right?

Okay, time for another fish tale!

The next critter in the Tudes' Hall of Champions wasn't fast like Rippy, powerful like Jim
Teal or strong like the To-Do-Wrights. But Harvey belongs on the Tudes' Hall wall with the rest
of the best!

59

Harvey Mertzy was a mollusk. He had a hard shell and crawled like a snail, leaving a trail of slime everywhere he went. I guess that's why the fish who didn't know him steered clear of him and called him names.

"Look out! It's that stinky slime-meister, Harvey Mertzy. Peeee-uuuuuu!"

"Yeah, don't touch what Harvey's touched or you're likely to get slimed. Mucus mollusk!" they teased.

But everyone who really knew Harvey loved him, because he was kind and compassionate.

Harvey came from the other side of the reef and lived in the grotto ghetto, south of town. The grotto was a tough place. His dad, Sho Kno Mertzy, had grown up there. Sho Kno drove a big 18-legged hermit-crab trailer across the ocean for a living and wasn't home much.

Harvey's dad had learned early in life to be hard and ruthless. Sho Kno thought you had to be tough to survive in the grotto.

But Harvey was different. He tried to help whenever he could. He didn't just see the needs of others—he felt them. When others hurt, he hurt. And lots of hurting fishfolk lived in the grotto. So many were homeless. So many had needs.

Carl Cucumber was caught in the currents with no place to stay. "Ouch! Owie! Umph! I'm getting all bruised and scraped up, rolling around in the grotto. I don't know what to do! Antoinette, can you help me get back on my feet?"

Antoinette Anemone sighed. "Carl Cucumber, you know that since I got washed off the reef I haven't found a place to call home. I can't help myself, let alone you. Ask Monte Man-of-War."

But Monte said, "Are you kiddin'? Yeah, I used to be a big-shot broker on Walrus Street—before my luck changed. I put all my money in bass bellies and they went belly up. I lost everything! Now I just drink suds with my buds to help me forget."

And then there was old Ollie. Oliver Octopus had been in the grotto longer than any of the other street critters. He was crustier than the crustiest crustacean.

He pushed a shopping cart around town with all his belongings in it, spewing dark ink on any fish who messed with him.

Old Ollie disliked everybody. But he especially hated do-gooder Harvey and called him names when he saw him. "Get out of my way, slimeball!"

Harvey hurt for his fellow fish—so badly, in fact, that he decided to do what he could to help. He prayed for them and much more. He collected cans and bottles for recycling and used the money to buy bandages for Carl Cucumber to wrap his cuts and bruises.

"Thank you, Harvey," Carl said gratefully. "You're one kindhearted mollusk!"

"Hey, Antoinette Anemone!" Harvey called one Saturday. "Get in my wagon. I'll tow you out to the reef and help you get established there. I know a great spot where you can feed yourself."

"Oh, thank you, Harvey!" she exclaimed.

Helping Monte was going to be tougher, but Harvey was a clever mollusk. Monte had a good head for business and Harvey knew it.

Harvey said, "Monte, let's collect bottles and cans and go to garage sales. We can use my wagon to move the stuff. We'll sell it for a fair price and buy more stuff. If we keep doing that, it won't be long until you can open your own secondfin store. You can call it Monte's Fresh Start Store: Giving Old Things Another Chance."

So they did. And now Monte Man-of-War tells all his customers, "Harvey Mertzy helped me get a new start in life. He's the best!"

But old Ollie felt differently. "I don't want no slimeball helping me. Get outta my face, Mertzy!"

One day, on his way home from school, Harvey saw Squid Squirt beating up Oliver Octopus two blocks away.

"Hey, leave him alone!" Harvey yelled. Harvey started toward them as fast as he could, but mollusks are awfully slow, you know.

After knocking Ollie to the sidewalk, the giant squid took off with Ollie's shopping cart. Thoroughly thrashed and thumped, Ollie looked around for help. "Squid Squirt has snatched my stuff!" he moaned.

Harvey was hurrying but still moving mighty slow when he saw Mayor Mackerel swim right past Ollie. The mayor crossed to the other side of the street and pretended not to notice the octogenarian octopus bleeding on the sidewalk. "I don't want to get involved," the mayor said to no one at all.

Oh no! The mayor didn't help, Harvey thought.

Harvey was about a block away when two highly respected evangelfish, Harold Hippocritter and Tuna Two-Face, spotted Ollie in distress. *Surely they'll help,* thought Harvey.

"I've got to get to my office," Hippocritter harumphed. "I'm preparing an important sermon on helping the poor. I don't have time to get involved."

"I have to hurry along, too," Two-Face trumpeted. "I'm doing lunch with a very wealthy donor."

Like the mayor, the evangelfish swam to the other side of the street, making a great effort to look anywhere but at the wounded octopus.

By the time Harvey got to him, Ollie was in pretty bad shape. There was a pay phone on the corner, and Harvey knew what to do. "I'll call 9-1-1."

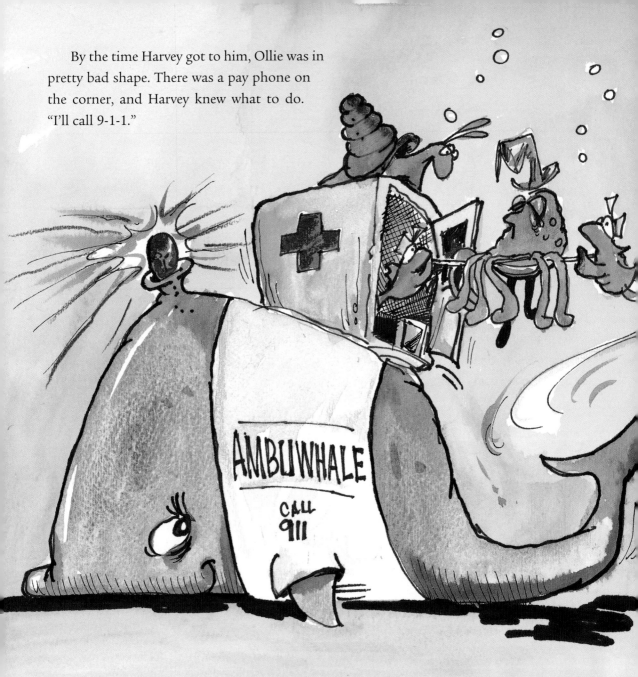

The ambuwhale arrived within five minutes with red lights flashing and siren blaring. Harvey held Ollie's head in his lap and wiped blood from his mouth as they rode to the fishpital. Ollie was unconscious.

The old octopus woke up a couple of times during the trip. The first time he tried to pull away, but the look in Harvey's eyes melted him. The second time Oliver awoke he didn't move. He even managed a smile when Harvey spoke.

"You'll be okay, Ollie. I'll help you."

"Soon you can leave, Ollie," Harvey said while visiting one day. "You've been in the fishpital two whole weeks!"

Ollie smiled weakly. "Yeah, and you've come to see me every day."

Ollie wasn't so crusty anymore—and he didn't even seem to mind Harvey's slime.

As he was leaving that day, Harvey swam into the fishpital chaplain.

"Chaplain Chad, you've been visiting Oliver Octopus, right?"

"Yes."

"Did he really say he might visit your church?"

"Why, yes, he did."

"Wow! Wouldn't that be great?" Harvey said.

"The Fishmaker can change anybody," Chaplain Chad smiled, "even Ollie."

"You're right! I'll be praying for him."

The next day Harvey went to see his friend Monte Man-of-War at the secondfin store. "Hey Monte, I need a favor. Oliver Octopus doesn't have any stuff. Would you donate a cart and a few things for when he gets out of the fishpital?"

"Sure, I would be glad to help him get a fresh start. Sometimes a fresh start is all it takes to make it."

The cart was a wonderful surprise to Ollie.

"You guys are great," Ollie said with a tear in his eye. "Thanks a lot!"

No, Ollie didn't leave the grotto. But he did change. He stopped calling Harvey a slimeball, and last I heard, ol' Oliver Octopus was starting to follow The Fishmaker.

I'm sorry to say that Harvey's dad never changed. Sho Kno didn't understand why Harvey wasn't tough like him, but young Harvey didn't live to make his dad happy and proud. He lived to please The Fishmaker.

The street critters loved Harvey, slime and all. Some of them even wrote to Fish University and told them about all he had done. Today, two words honoring Harvey Mertzy can be found in *Merriam-Lobster's Under-the-Bridge Dictionary*. Do you know the two words?

Have mercy . . . a pair of Harvey Mertzy words.

Mercy is what you feel for someone that leads you to help them, even when they don't deserve it.

When is the last time you showed mercy toward someone? What did you do?

If an adult were to go with you, is there someone in the hospital you can visit?

How has God been merciful to you? How can you show mercy to someone else?

When you pray today, tell God about the recent times you have failed to show mercy. Then thank Him for being merciful to you.

Thanks for spending this time with O. Whillikers. I love you a bunch!

The Tale of Toad Lee Purrhart, a Toad with a Pure Heart

Hey! Are you having a great day?  I'm having a dandy. And now I'm doing something I like best. I'm reading a story with you!

But before we go on, let's do a "think back."

Who was the marlin we read about?

Who was the porpoise?

Who was the eel?

Who were the stingrays?

Who was the mollusk?

Alrighty then! Nicely done. Now, how about a new tale? Bea and Atta Tude's Hall of Champions definitely has an international cast of characters. This story is about an amphibian from Asian waters. His name is Toad Lee Purrhart, and he has his mug on the wall in the hall, too.

Toad Lee Purrhart lived in the swamp at the lower end of China Lake. When he was your age, he moved around a lot and his folks didn't get along. And like the stingrays, Toad Lee had to untangle a web of double messages.

His dad, Notso Purrhart, was a gambler. Notso played poker and took bets on dragonfly races. He was well known as the swamp bookie.

"Dad, why do you take in all those bets? Isn't gambling against the law?"

"Hey, don't be a worrywart. It's okay, Son! So my business dealings are a little shaky. Some fish like to gamble a little and I help 'em, that's all. But I don't cheat anyone and I never tell lies—just like I taught you. Everyone knows Notso Purrhart is on the up and up."

"I know, Dad, but I do worry about you! This business is a little shady—"

"I said shaky, not shady!"

"Well, if it's shaky, then it's probably shady, too. Anyway, you're making a living by breaking the law, and that's not right."

Toad Lee knew that Grandpa Hard Lee had been tough on his father as a kid, but that was no excuse for his dad to be dishonest. "I get so confused," Toad Lee told his dad. "You tell me never to cheat or tell lies, but you say it's okay for you to break the law."

"We'll talk about this later, Son. Your friends are here to go to school. Hop to it and I'll see you this evening. Be cool after school . . . okay?"

"No sweat. Later, Dad. Hi, guys!"

74

Mocs Water Moccasin, Sandy Sand Dab and Shrimpy Shrimp were Toad Lee's best buddies. On the way to school they talked about what their dads did for a living.

Sandy said proudly, "My dad is in the Coast Guard and sails on China Lake. He's friends with Ken Catfish's dad who runs the J. Paul Guppy Museum of Fin Art. What about yours, Mocs?"

"Oh, he's an engineer. He shares bassball season tickets with Libby Leech's dad who manages that rock band The Traveling Whaleberries. How about yours, Shrimpy?"

"He's a reef estate broker. He just sold a huge home to Silvia Sucker's pop who sells used crab cars to suckers. What about your dad, Toad Lee? What does he do?"

Toad Lee Purrhart had hoped they wouldn't ask. He was embarrassed and just didn't know what to say—so he told the truth.

"Well . . . my dad runs the poker games in the back room of the Port Hole Sand Bar, and he takes bets on dragonfly races."

"Your dad's a bookie!" Sandy exclaimed. "Isn't that illegal?"

"Yeah, Sandy, it is."

"What does your mom say about that?" Mocs asked.

"My folks are divorced. I used to live with my mom, but now I live with my dad. My mom, Wuz Kno Purrhart, drinks a lot. And she was dating some real sea snakes. Even though my dad's a bookie, it's better living with my dad than with my mom."

"I'll bet that's hard for you," Shrimpy sympathized.

"It is. I love them both and they love me, but I don't want to be like them in their bad ways. I don't like how they live."

"How did you end up livin' with your dad, Toad Lee?" asked Sandy.

"Well, when my mom's drinking got worse, I started waking up in the mornings and finding different critters in our home."

"I'll bet that was awful."

"It was, Shrimpy. Then one morning there was Leon Leech."

"Leon Leech! What a creep!"

"I know. That was the last straw for me. I made the hardest decision of my life. That night I said, 'Mom, I love you very much, but I don't like all the drinking and these strange critters hanging around all the time. It's not right. Would you let me go and live with my dad?' She cried, but she let me go."

"How is it different with your dad?" Mocs asked.

"Well, Mocs, at first he lived with Tilly Tadpole, even though they w
was the same person with him all the time. That didn't make it right, bu
And even though they both smoked three packs of seaweeds a day, which
weren't drinking a lot or having wild parties."

"What's it like to come home from school to an empty pool?" Sandy w

"It's easy to get into trouble. With no adults around, I have to be care
hang with."

"Hey, Toad Lee, wassup, dude!" Some tough-looking fish were calling from the steps as the four friends arrived at school.

Mocs said warily, "What do they want, Toad Lee? Aren't those guys bad news?"

"It's okay. I know them, Mocs. Sometimes they get into trouble at school, but they're not all bad."

"All the same, I think we'll go in the other way," Mocs said. "Come on, guys. See you later, Toad Lee."

"Hey, dudes! Paul Perch, whacha' doin'?" Toad Lee greeted the gang.

"Hey, Toad Lee! Since no one's home, let's go to your pool after school! I've got some seaweed we can smoke and Billy Bluegill's got a *Mermaid* magazine."

"No way! Not at my pool. I wanna stay cool."

Toad Lee had a pure heart and he planned to keep it that way.

80

After school, Toad Lee decided he had to talk to his dad. Instead of going straight home, Toad Lee hopped over to the Port Hole Sand Bar. He thought this talk with his dad might be as hard as the talk he had with his mom. Maybe harder.

"How was school today?" his dad asked.

"Not so good."

"You look bummed, Son. What happened to get you down? Something bothering you?"

"The kids at school were talking about what their dads do for a living. Dad, this is hard to say, but I'm embarrassed by what you do. It's illegal and it's not right. I want you to know that I love you, but it would be great if I could be proud of what you do. Are you mad at me for saying that?"

Notso Purrhart shook his head. "No, Son. I'm not mad. I knew you didn't care for my business, but I sure didn't know you felt so strongly about it."

"And Dad," Toad Lee said, his courage growing, "I'd like to do something helpful for the family besides cleaning the bookie joint on Saturdays. I don't want to help you do what's wrong anymore."

Toad Lee held his breath. He didn't know what would happen next. Some dads hit when they're mad. Notso had never laid a hand on his son, but Toad Lee was afraid his dad would be really mad this time.

Notso surprised his son. First, he hopped over and hugged his only toad. "You're right, Son," he said. "I'm sorry I haven't been a very good example. My son's respect is more important than money. Tell you what, I'm gonna give up gambling and get a different job—one you'll be proud of. And speaking of changes, maybe it's time Tilly and I got married. I might even quit smoking! Don't hold me to it, but I'll give it a try."

You could have knocked Toad Lee over with a featherfish. Notso wasn't a liar. He always did what he said. And he promised to change—just because his son had the courage to share his pure heart.

Notso changed jobs, married Tilly and even quit smoking. But poor Tilly was hooked. She smoked three packs of Sail 'Em Seaweeds a day, and I'm sorry to say that she got gill cancer several years later. That's sad, but something good came out of it. Toad Lee had grown up by then to become Preacher Toad Lee Purrhart. He traveled the Pacific from coast to coast, telling fishfolk about The Fishmaker.

Well, Toad Lee told Tilly, and Tilly believed in The Fishmaker. When she died, she went to sea heaven. A few years later, ol' Notso got married again—to Polly Wog. He was still drinking a little, but one day Polly asked him, "You loved Toad Lee enough to quit gambling. Do you love me enough to quit drinking?"

Guess what? He hasn't had suds since. Wow! I guess you can teach an old toad new tricks!

Toad Lee's mom, Wuz Kno, had a hard life after Toad Lee moved out. She hit skid reef and suffered lots of grief. The years passed and one day she called her son after he had grown up. "Toad Lee, I've pretty well ruined my life up to now, but I'd like to know The Fishmaker and get right with Him. Would you help me?"

"I'd love to mom! Thanks for asking me."

What a surprise! Preacher Toad Lee Purrhart told her how to know The Fishmaker and she believed, too, just like Tilly. Afterward, Toad Lee's mom actually quit drinking for three years and even read the Living Sea Scrolls a lot before she died. Old toads *can* change.

The Merriam-Lobster editors at Fish University heard about how The Fishmaker used Toad Lee in the lives of his parents. And—you guessed 'er, Chester—they added a few new words to the dictionary:

Totally pure heart . . . Toad Lee Purrhart words.

Fishfolk who have pure hearts know right from wrong and choose to do right—even when those around them don't.

°TOTALLY PURE HEART°
—DO RIGHT...EVEN WHEN OTHERS DON'T—

Does anyone you know send you double messages? How can you help them give up their bad ways? Do you know God the way Tilly and Wuz Kno came to know The Fishmaker?

Now, how about having a nice talk with God? Visit with Him and ask Him to give you a pure heart. Ask Him how well you know Him.

O. Whillikers loves you . . . but not as much as God does.

Oh, one more thing. In case you haven't guessed, the tale I just told is also the life story of the man who wrote this book. Every part really happened, just like O. Whillikers told it. Only the names are different.

84

The Tale of Peaz Maukkar, the Peacemaker

Hi! It's time for another stroll down the Hall of Champions. Last time we talked about Toad Lee Purrhart. Do you remember the three words for which his name stands?

How about the other critters we've read about? Do you remember their names and what was special about them?

O. Whillikers has a dandy tale for you this time. This story is about a mako shark named Peaz Maukkar. Peaz migrated with his family from the Baltic Sea to a real tough part of Barracudaville, off the coast of Southern California. There the waters were calm and warm—unlike the Maukkar family.

Peaz's dad could be pretty mean. Trub L. Maukker lived up to his name. He would storm about the house, screaming at his wife, Homme Maukker, in front of the kids. Their house was not a very peaceful place.

"I hate my stinking job! I hate my boss! He's always yelling at me. I can't yell back 'cause I might get fired. So I yell at home. And if you don't like it, you can lump it!"

"Hi, Dad," Peaz said pleasantly. "Tough day at work, huh?"

"I've got a pansy for a son. What a wimp! Why aren't you out kickin' some tail? When I was your age, I could hardly wait to thrash some deep sea bass."

"I'm not like you, Dad. That's not my style. Why do you always want to fight?"

"Because mako sharks are mean. It's just the way we are. Anyway, fightin' is fun."

"Not for me, Dad. I'd rather get along with everyone."

"You'll never survive thinking that way, Son. You gotta be tough. Like our neighbors, the Hammerheads and Shovelnoses."

"Aren't their kids in jail, Dad?"

"What do you know, anyhow? Hey, who's at the door? Why it's your weenie best buddy, Billy, the gentle basking shark. Get outta here both of ya! I'm tired of lookin' at ya."

"Hi, Billy," Peaz hurried his friend away.

Billy didn't mention Peaz's surly dad but said, "Let's cruise by the school playground and shoot some hoops. You still hopin' to get a scholarship to huck honeydews at Honeydew U.?"

"Yeah, I'm still hopin' my hoopin' will get me in."

"Uh-oh, Peaz. There's George Greatwhite—the biggest bully on the block!"

"Hey, there's Bobby Blue Shark. He's a really nice guy," Peaz said. "I hope George doesn't spot him. What is it with the Greatwhites? Why don't they like the Blues? My dad doesn't like them either."

"Hey, Peaz, look! It's your dad! Trub L.'s comin'."

"I was watchin' you out the window," Peaz's father bellowed. "I've told you before, don't get chummy with the Blues. I can't stand 'em. My grandpa hates 'em. My dad hates 'em. I hate 'em. And I expect you to hate 'em, too! I especially hate Birmingham B. Blue, and I don't want you gettin' friendly with his son. Understand?"

"But Dad, aren't all fish the same in The Fishmaker's eyes?"

"Don't get religious on me, Peaz! Just stay away from the Blues. I'll see you later."

"I don't get it, Peaz."

"Me neither, Billy. I'm glad Bobby Blue is in our class at school. I like him."

"Me, too. So why does George Greatwhite try to pick on him?"

"I don't know, but Bobby doesn't take it. That's why George ends up picking on Steve Stinkybottom."

"Why poor Steve?" Billy asked.

"Billy, I think George picks on Steve because he's the only nonshark in the neighborhood."

"Yeah. And because Steve's a smelt."

"I suppose. He is a bottom fish, and he doesn't smell too good. Have you noticed how much time he spends by himself? He must be lonely."

"Peaz, it's not right to hate someone because of the kind of fish he is."

"You're right, Billy. But try telling that to George Greatwhite."

Everyone knew that George Greatwhite would hang out in the restroom at school, waiting to ambush Steve Stinkybottom and steal his lunch money. The schoolfish hated to go in there because of George and his friends. He was pretty chummy with the makos, and they made life tough on the other young sharks.

Shark Elementary was a tough school. The bathroom wasn't safe and neither was the playground. The makos and the whites would start fights with Bobby and the other blue sharks at recess, lunchtime, after school—any time the teachers weren't looking. You could always hear George and his buddies and Bobby and his friends yelling at each other until a full-fledged fight broke out.

"Blues eat fish eggs!"

"Oh yeah, well you're a stinkin' whitefish. And makos are minnow munchers!"

After yelling awhile, someone would throw a clam or oyster or scallop. Then with fins flashing and teeth gnashing, the fighting would begin. Peaz Maukkar and Billy Basking Shark wanted nothing more than to stop it somehow, but they didn't know where to begin.

"Wow! Look at those guys, Billy. They're fighting again. Do you think there's anything we can do?"

"There's too many for us, Peaz. We might as well go huck honeydews in the gym."

Shark Elementary was the only school in town without a honeydew team. Hucking honeydew melons is the national sport in Pacifica, and Peaz was a pretty good honeydew hucker.

Other schools hucked honeydews. The Whales were big but slow. The Porpoises were fast and small. The Orkas were both big and fast—and rough, too. But the Sharks didn't have a team.

Not having a team to play on was one of Peaz Maukkar's biggest disappointments when he moved to Barracudaville. He dreamed of hucking honeydews for the team at Honeydew U. And if he practiced hard, maybe he would be good enough to play professionally someday for the Lakers. Peaz was a big fan and collected Fishilicious trading cards of pro hucksters.

One day Peaz Maukkar and gentle Billy Basking Shark were looking through their cards and came across a retired player named Birmingham B. Blue. He had played for the Lakers and later coached at Fish U. Peaz was so excited he couldn't contain himself.

"Billy, that's Bobby's dad!"

"Wow, Dude! You mean Mr. Blue played for the Lakers?"

"Yeah, and he coached at Fish U. He's probably an old hobbled huckster by now, but maybe he could coach the Sharks. Let's go see him!"

89

Birmingham B. Blue was happy to meet the young honeydew fans, even if one of them was a mako. Peaz Maukker introduced himself and his friend Billy. "We wanted to ask if you'd be willing to coach a honeydew team at Shark Elementary. I'm a small forward and I shoot pretty well. My friend Bill would be a great power forward! George Greatwhite could be our center—he's big and tough. Your son Bobby would be a perfect point guard. He's 'lights out' when he shoots! And Steve Smelt is quick. He'd be super with Bobby in the backcourt. We might be pretty good. Besides, if you coach the Sharks, maybe the playground would be a more peaceful place—and the neighborhood, too. Maybe the sharks would stop fighting all the time."

Mr. Blue thought for a moment, then said, "You've shown a lot of courage coming here, Peaz. And you're very convincing. Okay, I'll give it a try. But you'll have to get the guys together. I suggest you talk to George first. We need a big center to go up against the Whales and the Orkas. I think he's a good place to start. But be sure to tell him that I'm going to coach. He may not be too happy to hear that."

"Okay, Mr. B.! Come on, Billy."

SURE...
I'LL PLAY

It wasn't long before they found George. The great white was hard to miss. "Hey, George, wait up!" Peaz called.

"What are you dingdongs doing here?"

Peaz said, "We're putting together a honey-dew team and we'd like you to be our center!"

"Oh yeah? You want me? I love to play!" Then George frowned. "Who's gonna be on this team?"

"Peaz and me," Billy spoke up.

"Yeah? You and who else?"

"Well, Steve Smelt and Bobby Blue will play guard. And Bobby's dad will be our coach."

"No way!" George protested. "I hate the Blues. And I don't like smelt."

Peaz said, "George, did you know that Birmingham B. Blue played for the Lakers?"

"Really! No kidding? I didn't know."

"Come on, George! It'll be great."

"Well, I guess I'm willing to try and see if it works. But it probably won't."

What are you Afraid of?

At first, Trub L. Maukkar forbid Peaz to play for the Sharks. He didn't want any Blue coaching his son. But Mr. Blue surprised Peaz's dad by asking him to help coach the team. Mr. Maukkar didn't want anything to do with the team, but he didn't want to look bad, so he said, "Yeah, I suppose I could help out some. If a Blue can coach, then I can, too."

After getting to know each other, the two dads actually got along. Trub L. Maukker found that Birmingham B. Blue was a real good guy.

"Birmingham, I sure was wrong about you," Trub told his new friend. "I guess I learned some things along the way that maybe weren't right. You're okay. Maybe what The Fishmaker says is true: No fish is better than any other fish."

"I've found that to be true often enough, Trub. Folks who don't like one another for the wrong reasons can end up being friends once they get to know each other. I'm glad we've become friends."

Things went pretty well after that. Even for Steve Smelt. After winning their first game, the guys threw Steve in the shower at the gym and wouldn't let him out until he tried using soap. Everyone laughed, including Steve. Steve Smelt liked having friends, and bathing seemed like a small price to pay. Besides, Cindy Sand Shark and Teri Tiger Shark started talking to him in the hall at school. He really liked that.

Bobby was a great passer and threw the ball to George a lot. George knew what to do with it and scored a bunch. After a game,

George spoke to Bobby.

"Thanks for dishin' the rock to me, Bobby. I admit I was wrong about a lot of things, including what I said about blue sharks. You guys are all right!"

The neighborhood was more peaceful, too. Getting the sharks off the streets and into the gym to huck honeydews and watch the games helped a lot.

As assistant coach for the Sharks, Trub L. Maukkar had something to take his mind off his troubles at work. As a result, he performed better on the job and he stopped yelling so much at home. His wife sure liked that. He even apologized to her and to his son.

"Will you forgive me? I'm so sorry for how I've behaved." Old sharks can change.

The Sharks beat the Whales and the Porpoises. But the Orkas were too much for them. Second place was a great start for a first-year team.

"We'll beat the Orkas next year, George."

"Yeah, Bobby, we'll get 'em next year. Gimme a high fin!"

Shark Elementary did so well in its first year of playing that *Honeydew Hucksters Illustrated* did a story on the team. George, Billy, Bobby, Steve and Peaz (their star player) were on the cover. Inside was a photo with Birmingham B. Blue and Trub L. Maukkar standing side by side, beaming with their fins around each other.

Fishweek magazine did a feature on solving the shark problem. The whole ocean saw that makos, great whites, blues, indeed sharks of all kinds could get along.

Peaz Maukkar was declared a hero. He went to Fishington, DC, where he received the Bi-Bells Peace Prize for bringing peace to his town. And he received the I. William Smellnomore Award for what he did for Steve Smelt.

Naturally, Fish University also honored Peaz Maukkar. What do you think his word is?

Peacemaker . . . a Peaz Maukkar word.

Peacemakers try to help troublemakers become friendmakers.

Guess who got the Uncle Ernie Award? Birmingham B. Blue, for being nice to someone who wasn't nice to him first.

And who do you think got a scholarship to huck honeydews at Honeydew U.? Why sure! Peaz Maukkar. No one deserved it more.

Are you usually a troublemaker or a peacemaker?

When is the last time you caused trouble?

Can you think of ways to help bring peace between your friends at school or among your family at home? Why don't you talk about that for a while?

Be sure and pray about the things you just talked about. Ask God to show you how to be a peacemaker.

Oh, did you know that O. Whillikers used to be a pretty fair honeydew hucker? I was. I even played on the Lakers with Birmingham B. Blue. But that was a long time ago!

The Tale of Percy O. T. Cod,
a Persecuted Codfish

Howdy! I have mixed feelings about this next story. I'm a little sad because this is our last tale. But I'm also excited because I think this story is the best one yet!

But first let's think back one last time. You should be able to tell me the kinds of critters we've read about in the first seven stories, their names and the words that describe their character. Can you?

Good! Okay, it's tale time.

There are two groups of fishfolk who get picked on the most: big shots and little shots. Some fishfolk pick on "biggies" because they want to bring 'em down. Other critters pick on the "littles" to make themselves feel big. This story is about picking on folks and getting picked on. It's about how a critter named Percy Q. T. Cod got his whole family immortalized in Bea and Atta Tude's Hall of Champions.

The COD FAMILY

"I'm tired of gettin' picked on," Percy complained to his friend Connie one day. "So I'm a codfish. So I'm ordinary and average. Is that any reason for the other fish to pick on me? I wish I was something more exotic—maybe a coho salmon like your grandma or a walleyed pike like your grandpa."

"Well, Percy, being half-Coho and half-Walleye made my mom a CoWall. When she married a muskie, I became a Cowalski. I don't mind, but some fish make fun of me because my name ends in 'ski.' They tell jokes about me and call me stupid. So be careful about what you wish for."

"I don't get it, Connie. What's in a name that makes one fish pick on another fish because of it?"

"You got me."

Another day, Percy told Connie, "Sometimes I wish I was a sunfish. The Fishmaker outdid Himself when He made them! I think they're the most beautiful fish in the sea. Sammy Sunfish lives in a great part of the reef. His family has plenty of clams and they live in an unbelievable cave filled with stuff. Sammy always rides the latest umpteen-speed seahorse. He's the coolest in his expensive shades, and he listens to the hottest music on his Stony SwimMan."

"Yeah, but I know lots of fish at school who don't like Sammy. I guess they resent him because he has so much stuff. The other fish pick on him almost as much as they pick on us."

Percy said, "Do you know who's the worst? It's that Billy Bigotfish. He's mean! I saw him spray paint Sammy's bicycle seat."

"He's mean to me too, Percy. I cried when he told a Cowalski joke in front of my friends at recess."

"That's tough, Connie. Yesterday, Billy yelled 'Yoo-hoo' while he smeared fish goo on my locker at school.

Then he and his bigot buddies called me names when I swam away."

That's about when Percy and Connie got together with Sammy Sunfish and came to see me, O. Whillikers! They heard this walrus knew someone who might be able to help.

"Hey, dudes and dudette!" I greeted the young friends. "I heard Billy and his bigot buddies have been picking on my pals. Come with me. There's a fish I want you to meet. I think he can help you deal with Billy."

"I have a question."

"Yes, Sammy."

"Where are we going?"

"To the Garden of Anemone to meet Sonfish Sunfish. You'll like him a lot!"

"What does this have to do with me?" Connie asked. "I'm not a sunfish. I'm a Cowalski."

"Be patient, Connie. My friend really loves Cowalskis."

"Well, what about me?" Percy piped up.

"He thinks codfish are very special, too."

"He does?"

SURE!

101

"Let me ask you a question on our way," I said. "Connie, if you were The Fishmaker and you wanted to be friends with the fish you'd made, how would you do it?"

"As The Fishmaker, I could do anything I wanted. So I guess I would command them to like me."

"What do you think, Sammy?" I asked.

"I'd only make the fish I wanted to—like me. Some fish I just don't like."

"How about you, Percy? What would you do?"

"You can force fishfolk to do lots of things, but you can't make 'em like you. The Fishmaker couldn't command us to like Him, even if He wanted to. Otherwise, we wouldn't be fish—we'd be robots."

"You're right, Percy. Very good! So how would you do it? How would you make friends with the fish?"

"I guess I would become a fish and see which ones liked me."

"Connie, why the sourpuss?" I said.

"Come on, O. Whillikers. Get serious. Why did you bring us here?"

"You've all heard about The Fishmaker—the God of Sea Heaven? Well, I know His Son, Sonfish Sunfish, and He wants to meet you. That's why I brought you here. What's wrong, Connie?"

"O. Whillikers, I'm not into this. How do you feel about it, Sammy?"

"I think you ought to chill a bit, Connie. I'm feelin' curious. Hey, O-Dude, is this where we're goin'? Is this the Garden of Anemone?"

"It sure is, Sammy. Hello, Sonfish, I'm here with the friends I told you about."

"Just a second, I'll be right there," came a voice from the garden. Then my friends caught their first glimpse of the Sonfish.

"Whoa! Check Him out!" Sammy gasped. "Regal to the max. What do you think, Percy?"

"I'm impressed, Sammy. What do you think, Connie?"

"Oh my gosh!" was all she could say.

"Not exactly, Connie," Sonfish said. "I am the Son of the God of Sea Heaven. So I guess that makes Me the Son of G.O.S.H. But since you don't know Me, I am not yet yours, so The Fishmaker is not your G.O.S.H. either."

"Uh, err, um . . . that was just an expression. I didn't mean anything by it," Connie stammered. "Lots of fish say 'Oh my gosh' all the time."

"Well, maybe they shouldn't. Say, do any of you want to meet The Fishmaker?"

"Sure!"

"Can we?"

"Cool!"

"Well, if you want to get to know Him, you must first get to know Me. Who did O. Whillikers say that I am, Percy?"

"He says you are The Fishmaker's Son."

"Percy, who do you say that I am?"

"I believe you are The Fishmaker's Son, too. And I want you to introduce me to The Fishmaker."

"Oh, give me a great big break!" Sammy steamed. "This guy's just a shiny sunfish. He's not the Son of The Fishmaker. He's not the God of Sea Heaven. Percy, you're nothin' but a stupid codfish. Connie, am I right or what?"

"I'm with you, Sammy. Percy, get a life! That sunfish dude gives me the creeps. I'm outta here."

"I'm just as big a deal as He is," Sammy boasted. "A sunfish is a sunfish is a sunfish. Wait up, Connie, I'll swim home with you."

Now, I had heard fish dis the Sonfish before, but Percy couldn't believe it. "Sammy and Connie just gave Sonfish the old flipper flip-off! And they're calling me names and picking on me just because I believe Sonfish is The Fishmaker's Son."

"I know, Percy. I'm sorry. Some fish choose not to believe—and they make fun of those who do believe. I get teased, too."

The next day at school was tough for Percy. Not only did he have to watch out for Billy and the bigots, but Connie and Sammy were picking on him, too—just because he was a believer.

"Hi, Connie. Hello, Sammy." Percy tried to be pleasant.

"You fool!" Sammy snorted. "That ol' Sonfish is just another fish."

"Don't speak to me, you stupid Sonfish follower," Connie scowled.

"But guys, knowing Sonfish is the only way to know The Fishmaker."

"I can't believe you fell for that line!" Connie laughed.

"Hook, line and sinker!" Sammy howled. "Hang it in your gill, codfish!"

And with that they turned tail and swam away.

That same day I heard a lot of yelling and swearing in the park. Billy Bigotfish and his buddies had Sonfish Sunfish hanging on a fisherman's stringer and were hoisting him up the flagpole of an old sunken ship. "Hit him!" they were shouting. "String him up!"

When they spotted me heading for the ship, Billy Bigotfish told his buddies to stop me. "He's trying to help the Sonfish! Throw him down and don't let him up until this is over."

I could see Sonfish had been badly beaten, and now, with the stringer through His gills, He couldn't breathe. Connie and Sammy were there, staring at the spectacle. Sammy hated Him— you could tell by his eyes. But Connie saw Sonfish looking directly at her, and her face softened. She listened as He gently spoke a few final words to her. I couldn't hear what He said, but I'll never forget the look in her eyes as He died.

Billy and the bigots had Sonfish Sunfish mounted and placed in the center of the park. Someone made a sign that read, "This is what happens to sunfish who claim to be The

Fishmaker's Son." An armed carp kept watch.

Connie had been crying for three days. As she wiped another tear away, she said to herself, *I've got to pull myself together. But that look and those eyes and His words. I can't get Him out of my mind. I've got to go back to the park and see Him one last time.*

But when she got to the park, she could hardly believe her eyes. "Oh, no!" she cried. "He's gone! I'd better get my tail over to O. Whilliker's place and tell him. I hope Percy is there. He needs to know, too!"

Percy was indeed at my place. We were sad about losing Sonfish. Suddenly, Sonfish swam right through the door—without even opening it!

"Wow! How'd you do that?" Percy asked, staring.

"Hi, Percy. How's it going, O.?"

"Awesome! Oh, Sonfish, we thought you were dead. What happened?"

"O. Whillikers, when you are the Son of The Fishmaker, not even death can keep you down." That's when Connie showed up, pounding on the door. As I opened it, she burst in yelling.

"Sonfish is gone! Sonfish is—"

"Connie, your gills are gaping," Sonfish said, smiling.

"Oh my gos— I mean, Oh my God of Sea Heaven. It's Him . . . er, I mean it's You!" Laughing and crying, Connie hugged Him hard and held on tight. You could tell she loved Him, too.

Let me make a long story short. When they were old enough, Percy and Connie got married. They had a couple of little Codwalskis and became missionaries. They took the Living Sea Scrolls to South America to tell the ferocious piranhas about Sonfish Sunfish.

And yes, many of the piranhas picked on Percy, Connie and their hatchlings. But Percy and Connie knew that being able to tell others about The Fishmaker was worth it.

Just like Percy Q. T. Cod, yours truly, O. Whillikers, gets picked on for what he believes and for telling other fishfolk about his friend Sonfish. But I think it's worth it. What do you think? Do people ever pick on you because of what you believe?

Because of all he went through, Percy Q. T. Cod got a word named after him in *Merriam-Lobster's Under-the-Bridge Dictionary*. Can you guess it?

Persecuted . . . a Percy Q. T. Cod word. It's a word that means getting picked on.

But Percy and Connie and the whole family got their pictures on the wall in the Hall—including their kids, Quentin and Tom. And now you know what Percy's middle initials stand for, don't you?

And guess who got the Uncle Ernie award? Me! Old O. Whillikers got it for having the courage to tell my friends about Sonfish Sunfish.

Who did God give to you instead of Sonfish Sunfish? Do you know God's Son like Percy and Connie knew Sonfish Sunfish? Are you willing to be picked on for talking about Jesus?

The next time you pray, ask God to give you the strength to be faithful, even when you're picked on. And if you are not yet a believer, would you invite Jesus into your life right now?

If you mean it, pray these words: "Lord Jesus, come into my life. I want to be friends with you and I want you to introduce me to your Father and have Him be my God."

Did you mean it? Great! I couldn't be happier for you. Now tell the person who gave you this book what you've done.

That's it! That's all there is. It's been fun!

O. Whillikers is praying you'll become the person God wants you to be. Do your part and He'll do his.

Remember, I love you very much. But not nearly as much as God does!

From the Living Sea Scrolls

(For Fishfolk Only)

Like Hugh Mills, happy are the humble, for they will swim without fear forever.

Like Rippy Tance, happy are the repentant, for they do not swim with a guilty conscience.

Like Jim Teal, happy are the gentle, for they can swim wherever they want.

Like the To-Do-Wright Brothers, happy are those who love to do right, for they can swim completely contented.

Like Harvey Mertzy, happy are the merciful, for they will be helped when they hurt.

Like Toad Lee Purrhart, happy are the pure in heart, for they understand the reason for doing right.

Like Peaz Maukkar, happy are the peacemakers, for they will be a part of The Fishmaker's family.

Like Percy Q. T. Cod, happy are those who are persecuted for doing right, for they will swim without fear forever.

MACKEREL 5:3-10

God Said It Like This for You and Me

Blessed are the poor in spirit, for theirs is the kingdom of heaven.

Blessed are those who mourn, for they will be comforted.

Blessed are the meek, for they will inherit the earth.

Blessed are those who hunger and thirst for righteousness, for they will be filled.

Blessed are the merciful, for they will be shown mercy.

Blessed are the pure in heart, for they will see God.

Blessed are the peacemakers, for they will be called sons of God.

Blessed are those who are persecuted because of righteousness, for theirs is the kingdom of heaven.

MATTHEW 5:3-10

About the Author

Jay Carty was raised in a broken home as an "at-risk kid." He played basketball at Oregon State University and later coached there before joining John Wooden's coaching staff at UCLA, where he coached Kareem Abdul-Jabbar. Jay also played pro basketball for the Los Angeles Lakers. He is now the director of Yes! Ministries and has committed his life to helping people say yes to God.

Calling Jay an unusual communicator is a mild understatement. Maybe a little nuts would be more accurate. Certainly off-the-wall! Not exactly a preacher or a teacher, Jay is more of a storyteller but with a very important message. Traditional, he is not. Challenging, he is. Jay's "stuff" is an unusual blend of humor and content. Kids don't nod off, and neither do their parents.

Jay speaks in churches, colleges, schools and retreat centers across the country. He has appeared on CBN, TBN and numerous radio and television shows, including "Focus on the Family" with Dr. James Dobson, and he is a speaker for Focus on the Family conferences.

Jay is the author of seven books including *Counterattack, Something's Fishy, Playing with Fire, Playing the Odds, Discovering Your Natural Talents* and *Only Tens Go to Heaven*.

Jay and his wife, Mary, make their home in Santa Barbara, California, where Jay is learning to surf. They have two grown children, two grandchildren (Anna and Matthew, pictured below) and a closetful of Hawaiian shirts—because that's what you wear in Santa Barbara.